The Silly Little Book

of

Monster
JOKES

The Silly Little Book
of
MONSTER
JOKES

mustard

This edition published and distributed by Mustard, 1999

Mustard is an imprint of Parragon

Parragon
Queen Street House
4–5 Queen Street
Bath BA1 1HE

Produced by Magpie Books, an imprint of
Robinson Publishing Ltd, London

Copyright © Parragon 1999

All rights reserved. This book is sold subject to the condition
that it shall not, by way of trade or otherwise, be lent, re-sold, hired
out or otherwise circulated in any form of binding or cover other than
that in which it is published and without a similar condition including
this condition being imposed on the subsequent purchaser.

ISBN 0 75253 008 9

A copy of the British Library Cataloguing-in-Publication Data
is available from the British Library

Printed and bound in Singapore

Contents

Introduction

We all know that there is no such thing as monsters, at least that's what we hope! But judging from the hilarious stories and cracking gags in these pages it seems the supernatural are a lot more fun than they look. But don't worry; you can always tell if there's a monster in your bedroom – he's the one with the M on his pajamas.

Monster Medley

Cross-Eyed Monster: When I grow up I want to be a bus driver.
Witch: Well, I won't stand in your way.

What do you call a mouse that can pick up a monster?
Sir.

What is the best way to speak to a monster?
From a long distance.

What does a polite monster say
when he meets you for the first
time?
Pleased to eat you!

Why did the monster-breeder call
his monster Fog?
Because he was grey and thick.

How do you tell a good monster
from a bad one?
If it's a good one you will be able to
talk about it later!

Why didn't the monster use
toothpaste?
Because he said his teeth weren't
loose.

How do you stop a monster digging
up your garden?
Take his spade away.

What do you call a monster with a
wooden head?
Edward.

What do you call a monster with
two wooden heads?
Edward Woodward.

What do you call a monster with
four wooden heads?
I don't know but Edward Woodward
would.

Why did the two cyclops fight?
They could never see eye to eye
over anything.

What happened when two huge
monsters ran in a race?
One ran in short bursts, the other
ran in burst shorts.

What kind of monster can sit on
the end of your finger?
The bogeyman.

What can monsters do that you
can't do?
Count up to 25 on his fingers.

Why did the monster cross the road?
He wanted to know what it was like to be a chicken.

What do you give a monster with big feet?
Big flippers.

How do you know when there's a monster under your bed?
Your nose touches the ceiling.

How do you know if there's a monster in your bed?
By the "m" on his pajamas.

What do monsters play when they are in the bus?
Squash.

How do you get six monsters in a biscuit tin?
Take the biscuits out first.

What's the difference between a
monster and a fly?
Quite a lot really.

Who won the Monster Beauty
Contest?
No one.

What happened when the nasty
monster went shoplifting?
He stole a free sample.

What happened when the nasty
monster stole a pig?
The pig squealed to the police.

What happened when the big,
black monster became a chimney
sweep?
He started a grime wave.

What do you call a huge, ugly, slobbering, furry monster with cotton wool in his ears?
Anything you like – he can't hear you.

How do you know if a monster is musical?
He's got a flat head.

What do you call a Mammoth who conducts an orchestra?
Tuskanini.

What aftershave do monsters wear?
Brute.

How can you tell if a monster has a glass eye?
Because it comes out in conversation

What did one of the monster's
eyes say to the other?
Between us is something that
smells.

What happened when a monster
fell in love with a grand piano.
He said, "Darling, you've got lovely
teeth."

Why did the monster cross the road?
He wanted some chicken for his tea.

How do you talk to a giant?
Use big words.

How do you know that there's a monster in your bath?
You can't get the shower curtain closed.

Why couldn't Swamp Thing go to the party?
Because he was bogged down in his work.

What happened when the monster fell down a well?
He kicked the bucket.

How did the world's tallest monster become short overnight?
Someone stole all his money.

How do you greet a three-headed monster?
Hello, hello, hello.

Why was the monster standing on his head?
He was turning things over in his mind.

What happened when the monster stole a bottle of perfume?
He was convicted of fragrancy.

What should you do if a monster
runs through your front door?
Run through the back door.

How do you address a monster?
Very politely.

Why did the monster knit herself
three socks?
Because she grew another foot.

What is the best way to get rid of a demon?
Exorcise a lot.

What's a devil's picket line called?
A demon-stration.

What is the demons' favorite TV sit-com?
Fiends.

Why do demons and ghouls get on
so well?
Because demons are a ghoul's
best friend.

What do you call a demon who
slurps his food?
A goblin.

What do foreign devils speak?
Devil Dutch.

A little demon came running into the house saying "Mom, Dad's fallen on the bonfire!" Mom said, "Great, we'll have a barbecue."

What did the little demon do when he bought a house?
He called it Gnome Sweet Gnome.

What happened to the demon who fell in the marmalade jar?
Nothing, he was a jammy devil.

Why was the demon so good at cooking?
He was a kitchen devil.

What do demons have for breakfast?
Deviled eggs.

What do demons have on holiday?
A devil of a time.

When do banshees howl?
On Moanday night.

What does a headless horseman ride?
A nightmare.

Mommy monster: What are you doing with that saw and where's your little brother?
Young monster: Hee, Hee, he's my half-brother now.

Mommy monster: Did you catch everyone's eyes in that dress dear?

Girl monster: Yes, mom, and I've brought them all home for Cedric to play marbles with.

1st monster: I've just changed my mind.

2nd monster: Does it work any better?

1st monster: I have a hunch.
2nd monster: I thought you were a funny shape.

1st monster: I was in the zoo last week.
2nd monster: Really? Which cage were you in?

Boy: Do you like monsters?
Girl: Sometimes.
Boy: How do you mean?
Girl: The times when they're away.

Girl: Mom, mom a monster's just bitten my foot off.
Mom: Well, keep out of the kitchen, I've just washed the floor.

Boy: Dad, Dad, come out. My sister's fighting this ten foot gargoyle with three heads.
Dad: No, I'm not coming out. He's going to have to learn to look after himself.

The police are looking for a monster with one eye.
Why don't they use two?

How did the monster cure his sore throat?
He spent all day gargoyling.

1st monster: What is that son of yours doing these days?

2nd monster: He's at medical school.

1st monster: Oh, what's he studying?

2nd monster: Nothing, they're studying him.

Did you hear the joke about the two monsters who crashed?

They fell off a cliff, boom, boom.

Did you hear about the monster
who sent his picture to a lonely
hearts club?
They sent it back saying they
weren't that lonely!

Did you hear about the monster
who lost all his hair in the war?
He lost it in a hair raid.

Did you hear about the monster
who had eight arms?
He said they came in handy.

Did you hear about the monster
who had an extra pair of hands?
Where did he keep them?
In a handbag.

Did you hear about the man who took up monster-baiting for a living?
He used to be a teacher but he lost his nerve.

What game do ants play with monsters?
Squash.

How do you keep an ugly monster
in suspense?
I'll tell you tomorrow . . .

How do man-eating monsters
count to a thousand?
On their warts.

What do you call a one-eyed
monster who rides a motorbike?
Cycle-ops.

What do you get if you cross a
man-eating monster with a skunk?
A very ugly smell.

How did the midget monster get
into the police force?
He lied about his height.

What do young female monsters
do at parties?
They go around looking for edible
bachelors.

Monster: I've got to walk 25 miles home.
Ghost: Why don't you take a train?
Monster: I did once, but my mother made me give it back.

Did you hear about the monster who went to a holiday camp?
He won the ugly mug and knobbly knees competition and he wasn't even entered.

Why are monsters' fingers never
more than 11 inches long?
Because if they were 12 inches,
they would be a foot.

What time is it when a monster sits
on your car?
Time to get a new car.

How can you tell the difference between a monster and a banana? Try picking it up. If you can't, it's either a monster or a giant banana.

A monster walked into the council rent office with a $5 note stuck in one ear and a $10 note in the other. You see, he was $15 in arrears.

Did the bionic monster have a
brother?
No, but he had lots of trans-
sisters.

Did you hear about the monster
who was known as Captain Kirk?
He had a left ear, a right ear and a
final front ear.

Did you hear about the monster burglar who fell in the cement mixer?
Now he's a hardened criminal.

Why did the monster have to buy two tickets for the zoo?
One to get in and one to get out.

1st Monster: That gorgeous four-eyed creature just rolled her eyes at me!
2nd Monster: Well, roll them back again – she might need them.

What did the monster say when he saw Snow White and the Seven Dwarfs?
Yum, yum!

What kind of monster has the best hearing?
The eeriest.

Why did the cyclops apply for half a television license?
Because he only had one eye.

Did you hear about the stupid monster who hurt himself while he was raking up leaves?
He fell out of a tree.

Did you hear about the monster
with one eye at the back of his
head, and one at the front?
He was terribly moody because he
couldn't see eye to eye with
himself.

What did the angry monster do
when he got his gas bill?
He exploded.

Why did the wooden monsters
stand in a circle?
They were having a board meeting.

What did the shy pebble monster
say?
I wish I was a little boulder.

How do monsters count to 13?
On their fingers.
How do they count to 47?
They take off their socks and
count their toes.

Why are most monsters covered in wrinkles?
Have you ever tried to iron a monster?

Monster: I'm so ugly.
Ghost: It's not that bad!
Monster: It is! When my grandfather was born they passed out cigars. When my father was born they just passed out cigarettes. When I was born they simply passed out.

Why did the monster take a dead
man for a drive in his car?
Because he was a car-case.

What did they say about the
aristocratic monster?
That he was born with a silver
shovel in his mouth.

Why was the sword-swallowing
monster put in prison?
He coughed and killed two people.

What's the best way of stopping a
monster sliding through the eye of
a needle?
Tie a knot in his neck.

Why did the monster drink ten
liters of anti-freeze?
So that he didn't have to buy a
winter coat.

A little monster was learning to play the violin. "I'm good, aren't I?" he asked his big brother.

"You should be on the radio," said the brother.

"You think I'm that good?"

"No, I think you're terrible, but at least if you were on the radio, I could switch you off."

Did you hear about the Irish monster who went to night school to learn to read in the dark?

Mrs Monster to Mr Monster: Try to be nice to my mother when she visits us this weekend, dear. Fall down when she hits you.

What do you get if you cross a dinosaur with a wizard?
A Tyrannosaurus hex.

What do you call a wizard who lies on the floor?
Matt.

How did dinosaurs pass exams?
With extinction.

What do you call a team of vultures
playing football?
Foul play.

What did the skeleton say to his
girlfriend?
I love every bone in your body.

Terror Trio – King Kong, Nessie and the Yeti

What do you get if you cross King Kong with a snowman?
Frostbite.

What is as big as King Kong but doesn't weigh anything?
King Kong's shadow.

What kind of money do yetis use?
Iced lolly.

What do you get if you cross King
Kong with a watchdog?
A terrified postman.

What followed the Loch Ness
Monster?
A whopping big tail.

What did the Loch Ness Monster
say to his friend?
Long time no sea.

What's brown and furry on the inside and clear on the outside?
King Kong in clingfilm.

Can the Abominable Snowman jump very high?
Hardly – he can only just clear his throat!

Why didn't King Kong go to Hong Kong?
He didn't like Chinese food.

What happened to the big shaggy
yeti when he crashed through the
screen door?
She strained herself.

Why did King Kong paint the
bottoms of his feet brown?
So that he could hide upside down
in a jar of peanut butter.

What is big, hairy and can fly
faster than sound.
King Koncord.

Why is King Kong big and hairy?
So you can tell him apart from a
gooseberry.

How do you catch King Kong?
Hang upside down and make a
noise like a banana.

What do you get if you cross King
Kong with a budgie?
A messy cage.

What do you give a seasick yeti?
Plenty of room.

Where are yetis found?
They're so big they're hardly ever
lost.

What do you get if King Kong sits
on your best friend?
A flat mate.

What do you get if King Kong sits
on your piano?
A flat note.

What do you get if King Kong falls
down a mine shaft?
A flat miner.

Why shouldn't you dance with a
yeti?
Because if it trod on you you might
get flat feet.

What do you call a yeti in a phone
box?
Stuck.

What do you call a Scottish sea
monster who hangs people?
The Loch Noose Monster.

How did the yeti feel when he had flu?
Abominable.

What do you get if you cross a fashion designer with a sea monster?
The Loch Dress Monster.

If King Kong came to England why would he live in the Tower of London?
Because he's a beef-eater.

What do yetis eat on top of
Everest?
High Tea.

What should you do if you are on a
picnic with King Kong?
Give him the biggest bananas.

What do you do if you find King
Kong in the kitchen?
Just don't monkey with him.

What kind of man doesn't like to sit in front of the fire?
An Abominable Snowman.

Why was the Abominable Snowman's dog called Frost?
Because Frost bites.

What do Abominable Snowmen call their offspring?
Chill-dren.

Where do Abominable Snowmen go to dance?
To snowballs.

What did one Abominable Snowman say to the other?
I'm afraid I just don't believe in people.

What is the Abominable Snowman's favorite book?
War and Frozen Peas.

What did the Abominable
Snowman do after he had his
teeth pulled out?
He ate the dentist.

Why did the Abominable Snowman
send his father to Siberia?
Because he wanted frozen pop.

How does a Yeti get to work?
By icicle.

What does a Yeti eat for dinner?
Ice-burgers.

Why did King Kong join the army?
He wanted to know about gorilla
warfare.

What do you get if you cross King
Kong with a frog?
A gorilla that catches airplanes
with its tongue.

What business is King Kong in?
Monkey business.

What would you get if you crossed
King Kong with a skunk?
I don't know but it could always get
a seat on a bus!

Where does King Kong sleep?
Anywhere he wants to.

What happened when King Kong
swallowed Big Ben?
He found it time-consuming.

What is large, yellow, lives in
Scotland and has never been
seen?
The Loch Ness Canary

Which is the unluckiest monster in
the world?
The Luck Less Monster.

How can you mend King Kong's arm if he's twisted it?
With a monkey wrench.

Boy: Mom, why can't I swim in Loch Ness?
Mother: Because there are monsters in it.
Boy: But Dad's swimming there.
Mother: That's different. He's insured.

Did you hear the joke about the fierce yeti?
It'll make you roar.

Did you hear about the man who tried to cross the Loch Ness Monster with a goat?
He had to get a new goat.

Two policemen in New York were watching King Kong climb up the Empire State Building. One said to the other, "What do you think he's doing?"

"It's obvious," replied his colleague, "he wants to catch a plane."

What steps should you take if you see a dangerous yeti on your travels?

Very large ones.

What do you get if you cross the
Loch Ness Monster with a shark?
Loch Jaws.

Where do you find wild yetis?
It depends where you left them.

What do you get if you cross an
elephant with the abominable
snowman?
A jumbo yeti.

How do you communicate with the Loch Ness Monster at 20,000 fathoms?
Drop him a line.

Multicolored and hairy Monster Jokes

What do you do with a blue
monster?
Try and cheer him up.

What is big, hairy and bounces up
and down?
A monster on a pogo stick.

What's blue and hairy and goes
round and round?
A monster on a turntable.

What do you do with a green monster?
Put it in the sun until it ripens!

What do you get if you cross a giant, hairy monster with a penguin?
I don't know but it's a very tight-fitting dinner suit.

What do you get if you cross a long-fanged, purple-spotted monster with a cat?
A town that is free of dogs.

Which is the most dangerous animal in the Northern Hemisphere?
Yak the Ripper

How can you tell the difference between a rabbit and a red-eyed monster?
Just try getting a red-eyed monster into a rabbit hutch.

Two purple, hairy monsters were walking along the seafront and one said to the other, "It's quiet for Thanksgiving."

Why did the monster paint himself
in rainbow colors?
Because he wanted to hide in the
crayon box.

What's big, heavy, furry, dangerous
and has sixteen wheels?
A monster on roller-skates.

Why did the monster have green
ears and a red nose?
So that he could hide in rhubarb
patches.

What happens if a big, hairy monster sits in front of you at the cinema?
You miss most of the film.

Why was the big, hairy, two-headed monster top of the class at school?
Because two heads are better than one.

What happened when a purple-headed monster took up singing? He had a frog in his throat.

What did the big, hairy monster do
when he lost a hand?
He went to the secondhand shop.

Why did the fat, hairy, drooling
monster stop going out in the
sunshine?
He didn't want to spoil his looks.

Why did the monster dye his hair
yellow?
He wanted to see if blondes have
more fun.

Who is the smelliest, hairiest
monarch in the world?
King Pong.

Why are monsters big and hairy?
So that you can tell them apart
from gooseberries.

Why do monsters have lots of
matted fur?
Because they'd look silly in plastic
macs.

What's big, red and prickly, has three eyes and eats rocks.
A big, red, prickly, three-eyed, rock-eating monster.

Boy: Did you know you can get fur from a three-headed mountain monster?
Girl: Really? What kind of fur?
Boy: As fur away as possible!

What do you get if you cross a plum with a man-eating monster?
A purple people-eater.

Why did the big hairy, monster give up boxing?
Because he didn't want to spoil his looks.

What do you get if you cross a tall, green monster with a fountain pen?
The Ink-credible Hulk.

Boy Monster: You've got a face like a million dollars.
Girl Monster: Have I really?
Boy Monster: Yes – it's green and wrinkly.

What do you get if a huge, hairy monster steps on Batman and Robin?
Flatman and Ribbon.

Did you hear about the horrible, hairy monster who did farmyard impressions?
He didn't do the noises, he just made the smells.

1st Monster: That orange and red checked coat of yours is a bit loud.
2nd Monster: It's okay when I put my muffler on.

Monster
Munch

On which day do monsters eat people?
Chewsday.

What is a sea monster's favorite dish?
Fish and ships.

What kind of cocktails do monsters enjoy?
Ighballs.

What does a monster mom say to her kids at dinnertime?
Don't talk with someone in your mouth.

What did the monster want to eat in the restaurant?
The finger bowl.

How do you know if a monster's come round for tea?
There are muddy footprints on the carpet.

What do nasty monsters give each other for breakfast?
Smacks in the mouth.

What's the hardest part of making monster soup?
Stirring it.

What did the monster say when he ate a herd of gnus?
" . . . and that's the end of the gnus."

What did the monster say when he saw a rush-hour train full of passengers?
Oh good! A chew-chew train!

Where do greedy monsters find their babies?
Under the guzzle-berry bush.

Little monster: Mom I've finished. Can I leave the table?
Mommy monster: Yes, I'll save it for your tea.

Mommy monster: Agatha, how often must I tell you not to eat with your fingers.

Agatha monster: Sorry Mom.

Mommy monster: I should think so! Use a shovel like I do.

1st monster: Who was that lady I saw you with last night?

2nd monster: That was no lady, that was my lunch.

Little monster: Mom, why can't we have dustbins like everyone else?
Mother monster: Less talking, more eating please.

Little monster: Mom, Mom, what's for tea?
Mother monster: Shut up and get back in the microwave.

Why do waiters prefer monsters to flies?
Have you ever heard anyone complaining of a monster in their soup?

What will a monster eat in a restaurant?
The waiter.

Why was the horrible, big monster
making a terrible noise all night?
After eating Madonna he thought
he could sing.

Mommy monster: Don't eat that
uranium.
Little monster: Why not?
Mommy monster: You'll get
atomic-ache.

A monster walked into a hamburger restaurant and ordered a cheeseburger, fries and a chocolate milkshake. When he finished his meal he left $10 to pay the bill. The waiter, thinking that the monster probably wasn't very good at adding up, gave him only 50 cents change. At that moment another customer came in. "Gosh, I've never seen a monster in here before," he said. "And you won't be seeing me again," said the monster furiously, "not at those prices."

Why did the monster eat a lightbulb?
Because he was in need of light refreshment.

What happened to Ray when he
met the man-eating monster?
He became an ex-Ray.

What happened when the ice
monster ate a curry?
He blew his cool.

The vampire went into the Monster
Cafe. "Shark and chips," he
ordered. "And make it snappy."

What makes an ideal present for a monster?
Five pairs of gloves – one for each hand.

Why did the monster walk over the hill?
It was too much bother to walk under it.

Mr Monster: Oi, hurry up with my
supper.
Mrs Monster: Oh, do be quiet –
I've only got three pairs of hands.

Father monster: Johnny, don't
make faces at that man. I've told
you before not to play with your
food.

Waiter on ocean liner: Would you like the menu, sir?
Monster: No thanks, just bring me the passenger list.

Frankenstein

What's the difference between Frankenstein and boiled potatoes? You can't mash Frankenstein.

How does Frankenstein sit in his chair?
Bolt upright.

What did one of Frankenstein's ears say to the other?
I didn't know we lived on the same block.

What happened to Frankenstein's stupid son?
He had so much wax in his ears that he became a permanent contributor to Madame Tussaud's.

Who brings monsters' babies?
Frankenstork.

What happened when a vicar saw a zombie with nothing on his neck?
He made a bolt for it.

Who do zombie cowboys fight?
Deadskins.

What did the zombie's friend say
when he introduced him to his
girlfriend?
Good grief! Where did you dig her
up from?

Why did the zombie go to hospital?
He wanted to learn a few sick
jokes.

What do you call zombies in a
belfry?
Dead ringers.

What do you find in a zombie's
veins?
Dead blood corpuscles.

What's a zombie say when he gets
a letter from his girlfriend?
It's a dead-letter day.

Where do zombies go for cruises?
The Deaditerranean.

What did the zombie get his
medal for?
Deadication.

What happened to the zombie who
had a bad cold?
He said, "I'm dead-up wid fuddy
jokes aboud zondies."

What do little zombies play?
Corpses and Robbers.

Why was the zombie's nightclub a disaster?
It was a dead and alive hole.

How do you know a zombie is tired?
He's dead on his feet.

Why do zombies learn Latin and Greek?
Because they like dead languages.

What did Dr Frankenstein get when he put his goldfish's brain in the body of his dog?
I don't know, but it is great at chasing submarines.

How did Dr Frankenstein pay the men who built his monster?
On a piece rate.

Dr Frankenstein was sitting in his cell when suddenly through the wall came the ghost of his monster, with a rope round his neck.

Frankenstein said, "Monster, monster, what are you doing here?"

The monster said, "Well boss, they hanged me this morning so now I've come to meet my maker."

What happened to Frankenstein's
monster on the road?
He was stopped for speeding,
fined $50 and dismantled for six
months.

How did Frankenstein's monster
eat his lunch?
He bolted it down.

What does Frankenstein's monster
call a screwdriver?
Daddy.

What do you call a clever monster?
Frank Einstein.

What happened when the ice
monster had a furious row with the
zombie?
He gave him the cold shoulder.

What did Frankenstein's monster
say when he was struck by
lightning?
Thanks, I needed that.

Dr Frankenstein: Igor, have you seen my latest invention? It's a new pill consisting of 50 per cent glue and 50 per cent aspirin.
Igor: But what's it for?
Dr Frankenstein: For monsters with splitting headaches.

Dr Frankenstein: How can I stop that monster charging?
Igor: Why not take away his credit card?

Monster: Someone told me Dr Frankenstein invented the safety match.

Igor: Yes, that was one of his most striking achievements.

Monster Books and Knock Knock Jokes

What did the monster say when he
ate Aesop?
Make a fable out of that then!

What do ogres use to write with?
Ball point men.

The Bad-Tempered Werewolf – by
Claudia Armoff.

The Greediest Monster in the World – by Buster Gutt

The Monster Hanging off the Cliff – by Alf Hall

The Hungry Yeti – by Aida Lot

Tracking Monsters – by Woody Hurt

I Met An Abominable Snowman –
by Anne Tarctic

Monsters I Have Known – by
O. Penjaw

When to go Monster Hunting – by
Mae B. Tomorrow

Bungee Jumping with Monsters –
by Wade R. Go

A Very Hungry Giant – by Ethan
D. Lot

I Caught the Loch Ness Monster –
by Janet A. Big-Wun

Knock knock.
Who's there?
King Kong.
King Kong who?
King Kong's now part of China.

Knock knock.
Who's there?
Turner.
Turner who?
Turner round, there's a monster
breathing down your neck.

Knock knock.
Who's there?
Herman.
Herman who?
Herman Munster.

Knock knock.
Who's there?
Oliver.
Oliver who?
Oliver lone and I'm frightened of
monsters.

Knock knock.
Who's there?
Murphy.
Murphy who?
Murphy, have murphy! Don't eat
me!

Knock knock.
Who's there?
Cecile.
Cecile who?
Cecile th-the w-windows. Th-there
is a m-monster out there.

Knock knock.
Who's there?
Aida.
Aida who?
Aida whole village 'cos I'm a
monster.

Knock knock.
Who's there?
Adair.
Adair who?
Adair you to open this door and
see my fangs.

Knock knock.
Who's there?
Fido.
Fido who?
Fido known you were coming I'd
have bolted all the doors.

Knock knock.
Who's there?
Reuben.
Reuben who?
Reuben my eyes 'cos I can't
believe what a big monster you are.

Knock knock.
Who's there?
Teheran.
Teheran who?
Teheran very slowly – there's a
monster behind you.

Knock knock.
Who's there?
Chile.
Chile who?
Chile being an abominable
snowman!

Knock knock.
Who's there?
Kenya.
Kenya who?
Kenya save me from the
monsters?

Knock knock.
Who's there?
Ghana.
Ghana who?
Ghana get me a gun and shoot
that werewolf.

How to Feed Werewolves – by Nora Bone

What's a man-eating monster's favorite book?
Ghouliver's Travels.

What's a giant's favorite tale? A tall story.

Dracula

How do vampire footballers get the mud off?
They all get in the bat-tub.

What do you call a dog owned by Dracula?
A blood hound.

Why does Dracula have no friends?
Because he's a pain in the neck.

What did the vampire do to stop
his son biting his nails?
He cut all his fingers off.

What was the Californian hippie
vampire like?
He was ghoul man. Real ghoul.

What's a vampire's favorite sport?
Batminton.

What happened to the two mad vampires?
They both went a little batty.

What do vampires cross the sea in?
Blood vessels.

What do vampires have at eleven o'clock every day?
A coffin break.

Where do vampires go on holiday?
To the Isle of Fright.

What do vampire footballers have
at half-time?
Blood oranges.

What do vampires like that are red
and very silly?
Blood clots.

How does Dracula like to have his food served?
In bite-sized pieces.

What do vampires make sandwiches out of?
Self-raising dead.

Why did the vampire take up acting?
It was in his blood.

What is Count Dracula's least favorite song?
Vampire's Burning, Vampire's Burning.

What happened when a doctor crossed a parrot with a vampire?
It bit his neck, sucked his blood and said, "Who's a pretty boy then?"

Why did the vampire baby stop
having baby food?
He wanted something to get his
teeth into.

What happened to the lovesick
vampire?
He became a neck-romancer.

What do you get if you cross a
vampire with a snail?
I don't know but it would slow him
down.

Which vampire ate the three bears'
porridge?
Gouldilocks.

Which vampire tried to eat James
Bond?
Ghouldfinger.

Why did the vampire go to
hospital?
He wanted his ghoulstones
removed.

Why did the vampire stand at the bus-stop with his finger up his nose?
He was a ghoulsniffer.

What does a vampire say when you tell him a ghoul joke?
Ghoul blimey!

What's Dracula's favorite dance?
The fang-dango.

When do vampires bite you?
On Wincedays.

What's a vampire's favorite drink?
A Bloody Mary.

What do vampires think of blood
transfusions?
New-fang-led rubbish.

Why did the vampire enjoy ballroom dancing?
He could really get into the vaultz.

What happened at the vampires' race?
They finished neck and neck.

Where did vampires go to first in America?
New-fang-land.

What did Dracula say to the
Wolfman?
You look like you're going to the
dogs.

What do you get if you cross
Dracula with Al Capone?
A fangster.

Where do Chinese vampires come
from?
Fanghai.

What do vampires sing on New
Year's Eve?
Auld Fang Syne.

What do vampires have for lunch?
Fangers and mash.

What happened at the vampires'
reunion?
 All the blood relations went.

What is Dracula's favorite fruit?
Neck-tarines.

Why did Dracula go to the dentist?
He had fang decay.

Why did he have fang decay? He
was always eating fangcy cakes.

If you want to know more about
Dracula what do you have to do?
Join his fang club.

What is the American national day
for vampires?
Fangsgiving Day.

Why are vampire families so close?
Because blood is thicker than
water.

How do vampires keep their breath
smelling nice?
They use extractor fangs.

What does Dracula say when you
tell him a new fact?
Well, fangcy that!

Why was Dracula thought as being
polite?
He always said fangs.

Why did the vampire attack the clown?
He wanted the circus to be in his blood.

Did you know that Dracula wants to become a comedian?
He's looking for a crypt writer.

Which flavor ice cream is Dracula's favorite?
Vein-illa.

What is the first thing that
vampires learn at school?
The alphabat.

Why did Dracula go to the
orthodontist?
He wanted to improve his bite.

Why is Hollywood full of vampires?
They need someone to play the bit
parts.

Why do vampires like school dinners?
Because they know they won't get stake.

Why wouldn't the vampire eat his soup?
It clotted.

Why are vampires always exhausted in April?
Because they've just completed a long March of 31 days.

Why did the vampire sit on a
pumpkin?
It wanted to play squash.

What do you get if you cross
Dracula with a snail?
The world's slowest vampire.

What is a vampire's favorite soup?
Scream of tomato.

What's the difference between a
vampire and a biscuit?
Have you ever tried dunking a
vampire in your tea?

What do you get if you cross a
vampire with a jar of peanut
butter?
A vampire that sticks to the roof of
your mouth.

What do you get if you cross a Rolls-Royce with a vampire?
A monster that attacks expensive cars and sucks out their gas tanks.

How do you join the Dracula Fan Club?
Send you name, address and blood group.

What happened when two vampires
went mad?
They went bats.

What's the vampire's favorite
song?
Fangs for the Memory.

What's a vampire's favorite animal?
A giraffe.

What do you get if you cross
Dracula with Sir Lancelot?
A bite in shining armor.

Why was the young vampire a
failure?
Because he fainted at the sight of
blood.

Why did the vampire give up
acting?
He couldn't find a part he could
get his teeth into.

What happened to the vampire who
swallowed a sheep?
He felt baaaaaaaaaaaaaaad.

What does Mrs Dracula say to
Mr Dracula when he leaves for
work in the evening?
Have a nice bite!

What's Dracula's favorite coffee?
De-coffin-ated.

What's Dracula's car called?
A mobile blood unit.

Why do vampires do well at school?
Because every time they're asked
a question they come up with a
biting reply.

What is the vampire's favorite
slogan?
Please Give Blood Generously.

Why are vampires crazy?
Because they're often bats.

What did the vampire say when he
had been to the dentist?
Fangs very much.

What kind of medicine does
Dracula take for a cold?
Coffin medicine.

How does a vampire clean his house?
With a victim cleaner.

Where is Dracula's American office?
The Vampire State Building.

Where do vampires keep their savings?
In blood banks.

What does the postman take to vampires?
Fang mail.

What did the vampire sing to the doctor who cured him of amnesia?
Fangs for the Memory.

What does a vampire stand on after taking a shower?
A bat mat.

What's a vampire's favorite dance?
The Vaults.

What do romantic vampires do?
Neck.

Heard about the vampire who was
locked up in an asylum?
He went bats.

What do you call a vampire junkie?
Count Drugula.

What did the vampire call his false teeth?
A new fangled device.

What did Dracula say to his new apprentice?
We could do with some new blood around here.

Why do vampires hate arguments?
Because they make themselves
cross.

What happened when the vampire
went to the bloodbank?
He asked to make a withdrawal.

What's a vampire's favorite love
song?
How Can I Ignore the Girl Necks
Door.

What does a vampire say to the mirror?
Terror, terror on the wall.

What's a vampire's favorite cartoon character?
Batman.

What did Dracula call his daughter?
Bloody Mary.

Why do vampires eat in transport cafes?
He can eat for necks to nothing in them.

What type of people do vampires like?
O positive people.

What do vampires play poker for?
High stakes.

Werewolves

Mommy, Mommy, what's a
werewolf?
Shut up John and comb your face.

Why was the werewolf arrested in
the butcher's shop?
He was chop-lifting.

What parting gift did a mommy
werewolf give to her son when he
left home?
A comb.

Where does a werewolf sit in the theater?
Anywhere he wants to!

What do you get if you cross a witch with a werewolf?
A mad dog that chases airplanes.

What do you get when you cross a werewolf with a drip-dry suit?
A wash-and-werewolf.

What happened when the werewolf
chewed a bone for an hour?
When he got up he only had three
legs.

How do you know that a werewolf's
been in the fridge?
There are paw prints in the butter.

How do you know that two werewolves have been in the fridge?
There are two sets of paw prints in the butter.

What does it mean if there is a werewolf in your fridge in the morning?
You had some party last night!

Did you hear about the comedian
who entertained at a werewolves'
party?
He had them howling in the aisles.

Did you hear about the sick
werewolf?
He lost his voice but it's howl right
now.

Werewolf: Doctor, doctor, thank you so much for curing me.
Doctor: So you don't think you're a werewolf anymore?
Werewolf: Absolutely not, I'm quite clear now – see my nose is nice and cold.

What do you get if you cross a hairdresser with a werewolf?
A monster with an all-over perm.

What happened when the werewolf
swallowed a clock?
He got ticks.

How do you make a werewolf stew?
Keep him waiting for two hours.

Why did the boy take an aspirin
after hearing a werewolf howl?
Because it gave him an eerie
ache.

Why shouldn't you grab a werewolf by its tail?
It might be the werewolf's tail but it could be the end of you.

I used to be a werewolf but I'm all right nooooooooooooooooooow!

How do you stop a werewolf attacking you?
Throw a stick and shout fetch!

Why are werewolves thought of as quick-witted?
Because they always give snappy answers.

Why did the mommy and daddy werewolves call their son Camera?
Because he was always snapping.

What do you call a hairy beast with clothes on?
A wear-wolf.

What do you call a hairy beast in a river?
A weir-wolf.

What do you call a hairy beast that no longer exists?
A were-wolf.

What do you call a hairy beast that's lost?
A where-wolf.

What happens if you cross a
werewolf with a sheep?
You have to get a new sheep.

What's fearsome, hairy and drinks
from the wrong side of a glass?
A werewolf with hiccoughs.

What did the werewolf write at the
bottom of the letter?
Best vicious . . .

What happened when the werewolf met the five-headed monster?
It was love at first fright.

Monster: Where do fleas go in winter?
Werewolf: Search me!

How do you stop a werewolf howling in the back of a car?
Put him in the front.

Medical Moments

Monster: Doctor, doctor, how do I stop my nose from running?
Doctor: Stick out your foot and trip it up.

Doctor: You need new glasses.
Monster: How did you guess?
Doctor: I could tell the moment you walked through the window.

Doctor: I'm sorry madam, but I have to tell you that you are a werewolf.
Patient: Give me a piece of paper.
Doctor: Do you want to write your will?
Patient: No, a list of people I want to bite.

Monster: Doctor, doctor, what did the x-ray of my head show?
Doctor: Absolutely nothing.

Monster: Doctor, doctor, I need to lose 30 pounds of excess flab.
Doctor: All right, I'll cut your head off.

Monster: Doctor, doctor, I think I'm a bridge.
Doctor: What on earth's come over you?
Monster: Six cars, two trucks and a bus.

Monster: Doctor, doctor, I'm a blood-sucking monster and I keep needing to eat doctors.
Doctor: Oh, what a shame. I'm a dentist.

Monster: Doctor, doctor, how long can one live without a brain?
Doctor: That depends. How old are you?

Monster: Doctor, I have this irrepressible urge to paint myself all over in gold.
Doctor: Don't worry, it's just a gilt complex.

Doctor, I've just been bitten on the leg by a werewolf.
Did you put anything on it?
No, he seemed to like it as it was.

Doctor, doctor, I keep dreaming there are great, gooey, bug-eyed monsters playing tiddlewinks under my bed. What shall I do? Hide the tiddlewinks.

Monster: Doctor, doctor, I've got a split personality.
Doctor: Sit down, both of you.

Doctor, doctor, I keep thinking I'm the Abominable Snowman.
Keep cool.

Doctor: Did the mud pack help your appearance?
Monster: Yes, but it fell off after a few days.

A monster went to see the doctor because he kept bumping into things. "You need glasses," said the doctor.
"Will I be able to read with them?" asked the monster.
"Yes."
"That's brilliant," said the monster. "I didn't know how to read before."

Did you hear about the vain
monster who was going bald?
The doctor couldn't do a hair
transplant for him, so he shrunk
his head to fit his hair.

Did you hear about the snooker-
mad monster? He went to the
doctor because he didn't feel well.
"What do you eat?" asked the
doctor.
"For breakfast I have a couple of
red snooker balls, and at
lunchtime I grab a black, a pink

and two yellows. I have a brown with my tea in the afternoon, and then a blue and another pink for dinner."

"I know why you are not feeling well," exclaimed the doctor. You're not getting enough greens."

Slithering Slimies and Revolting Reptiles

What did the snake say when he was offered a piece of cheese for dinner?
Thank you, I'll just have a slither.

What did one slug say to another who had hit him and rushed off?
I'll get you next slime!

How do you know your kitchen is filthy?
The slugs leave trails on the floor that read "Clean me."

What did the slug say as he slipped down the window very fast?
How slime flies!

What's the difference between school dinners and a pile of slugs?
School dinners come on a plate.

What is the strongest animal in the world?
A snail, because it carries its home on its back.

What do you do when two snails
have a fight?
Leave them to slug it out.

What is the definition of a slug?
A snail with a housing problem.

Where do you find giant snails?
On the end of a giant's fingers.

What do you get if you cross a
worm with a young goat?
A dirty kid.

What do you get if you cross a
glow-worm with a pint of beer?
Light ale.

Why was the glow-worm unhappy?
Because her children were not very
bright.

What did the woodworm say to the chair?
It's been nice gnawing you!

What's worse than finding a maggot in your apple?
Finding half a maggot in your apple.

What did one maggot say to another?
What's a nice girl like you doing in a joint like this?

What do you get if you cross a glow-worm with a python?
A twenty-foot long strip-light that can squeeze you to death.

How can you tell if you are looking at a police glow-worm?
He has a blue light.

When should you stop for a glow-worm?
When he has a red light.

Why are glow-worms good to carry
in your bag?
They can lighten your load.

What's yellow, wiggly and
dangerous?
A maggot with a bad attitude.

What did one worm say to another
when he was late home?
Why in earth are you late?

What's the difference between a
worm and a gooseberry?
Ever tried eating worm pie?

What do you get if you cross a
worm with an elephant?
Big holes in your garden.

What is the best advice to give a
worm?
Sleep late.

Why do worms taste like chewing gum?
Because they're Wrigley's.

What lives in apples and is an avid reader?
A bookworm.

What makes a glow-worm glow?
A light meal.

What would you do if you found a bookworm chewing your favorite book?
Take the words right out of its mouth.

What is a bookworm's idea of a big feast?
War and Peace.

Who was wet and slippery and invaded England?
William the Conger.

What is wet and slippery and likes
Latin American music?
A conga eel.

What do you get if you cross a
snake with a Lego set?
A boa constructor.

What is a snake's favorite food?
Hiss fingers.

What is the difference between a poisonous snake and a headmaster?
You can make a pet out of the snake.

Which hand would you use to grab a poisonous snake?
Your enemy's.

What do you do if you find a black mamba in your toilet?
Wait until he's finished.

What is a snake's favorite opera?
Wriggletto.

Why did the two boa constrictors
get married?
Because they had a crush on each
other.

What should you do if you find a
snake in your bed?
Sleep in the wardrobe.

What do you call a snake that is
trying to become a bird?
A feather boa.

Why can't you trust snakes?
They speak with forked tongue.

What snakes are good at sums?
Adders.

What do you get if you cross a
snake with a hotdog?
A fangfurther.

What is a snake's favorite dance?
Snake rattle and roll.

What do you get if you cross a
snake with a pig?
A boar constrictor.

Why are snake's hard to fool?
They have no leg to pull.

What do you call a python with a
great bedside manner?
A snake charmer.

Why did the viper want to become
a python?
He got the coiling.

What do most people do when they
see a python?
They re-coil.

What school subject are snakes
best at?
Hiss-tory.

What did the snake say to the
cornered rat?
Hiss is the end of the line mate!

What do snakes have on their bath
towels?
Hiss and Hers.

What do you call a snake that
informs the police?
A grass-snake.

What did the python say to the
viper?
I've got a crush on you.

What did the mommy snake say to
the crying baby snake?
"Stop crying and viper your nose."

What's the best thing about
deadly snakes?
They've got poisonality.

What's the snakes' favorite
dance?
The mamba.

What's the snakes' second
favorite dance?
The shuffle.

What do you get if you cross two
snakes with a magic spell?
Addercadabra and abradacobra.

What did one snake say when the
other snake asked him the time?
Don't asp me!

What do you give a sick snake?
Asp-rin.

What would you get if you crossed
a new-born snake with a basket-
ball?
A bouncing baby boa.

What kind of letters did the snake
get from his admirers?
Fang mail.

What's long and green and goes
hith?
A snake with a lisp.

Why did some snakes disobey
Noah when he told them to go
forth and multiply?
They couldn't – they were adders.

Which snakes are found on cars?
Windscreen vipers.

What's the definition of a nervous breakdown?
A chameleon on a tartan rug.

What kind of tiles can't you stick on the wall?
Rep-tiles.

What do you call a rich frog?
A gold-blooded reptile.

What kind of bull doesn't have horns?
A bullfrog.

What jumps up and down in front of a car?
Froglights.

Where does a ten tonne frog sleep?
Anywhere it wants to!

When is a car like a frog?
When it's being toad.

What did one frog say to the other?
Time's sure fun when you're having flies!

What did the bus conductor say to the frog?
Hop on.

What do you say to a hitch-hiking frog?
Hop in!

Why did the toad become a lighthouse keeper?
He had his own frog-horn.

What do you call a frog who wants to be a cowboy?
Hoppalong Cassidy.

Why do frogs have webbed feet?
To stamp out forest fires.

What is a frog's favorite dance?
The Lindy Hop.

What do frogs sit on?
Toadstools.

What happens to illegally parked frogs?
They get toad away.

What do you say if you meet a toad?
Wart's new?

Why did the lizard go on a diet?
It weighed too much for its scales.

What's green and can jump a mile a minute?
A frog with hiccoughs.

What did the croaking frog say to his friend?
I think I've got a person in my throat.

What's green and goes round and round at 60 miles an hour?
A frog in a liquidizer.

What is yellow and goes round and round at 60 miles an hour?
A mouldy frog in a liquidizer.

Why was the frog down-in-the-mouth?
He was un-hoppy.

Why is a frog luckier than a cat?
Because a frog croaks all the time – a cat only croaks nine times.

How do frogs die?
They Kermit suicide.

Why doesn't Kermit like
elephants?
They always want to play leap-frog
with him.

What do you get if you cross a
planet with a toad?
Star warts.

What is a toad's favorite ballet?
Swamp Lake.

What do toads drink?
Croaka-cola.

What do frogs drink?
Hot croako.

What is green and slimy and is
found at the North Pole?
A lost frog.

What kind of shoes to frogs like?
Open toad sandals.

What do you call a frog spy?
A croak and dagger agent.

Where do frogs keep their treasure?
In a croak of gold at the end of the rainbow.

What do you get if you cross a toad with a mist?
Kermit the Fog.

What do you call a girl with a frog on her head?
Lily.

How did the toad die?
It simply croaked.

What is a cloak?
The mating call of a Chinese toad?

What's the weakest animal in the world?
A toad. He will croak if you touch him.

Where do toads leave their coats
and hats?
In the croakroom.

What is green and tough?
A toad with a machine gun.

What's white on the outside, green
on the inside and comes with
relish and onions?
A hot frog.

What happens if you eat a hot frog?
You croak in no time.

What is the chameleon's motto?
A change is as good as a rest.

What kind of pole is short and floppy?
A tadpole.

What do you call a skeleton snake?
A rattler.

Keeping Pet Snakes – by Sir Pent

Collecting Reptiles – by Ivor Frog

Collecting Wriggly Creatures – by
Tina Worms

There once was a snake named
Drake
Who started a fight with a rake.
It cut off his tail
Drake went very pale
And that's the short end of my
tale.

There was an old man called Jake
Who had a poisonous snake.
It bit his head
And now he's dead
So that was the end of Jake.

A boa with coils uneven
Had the greatest trouble in
breathing.
With jokes she was afflicted
For her laughs got constricted
And her coils started writhing and
wreathing.

A cobra was invited to dine
By his charmingly cute valentine.
But when he got there
He found that the fare
Was pineapple dumplings with
wine.

1st person: I've just been bitten by a snake on one arm.
2nd person: Which one?
1st person: I don't know, one snake looks very much like the next one.

Mother: John, why did you put a slug in auntie's bed?
John: Because I couldn't find a snake.

1st snake: I'm glad I'm not poisonous!
2nd snake: Why?
1st snake: Because I've just bitten my tongue.

Fisherman: What are you fishing for sonny?
Boy: I'm not fishing, I'm drowning worms.

Surveyor: This house is a ruin. I wonder what stops it from falling down?
Owner: I think the woodworm are holding hands.

Boy: What's black, slimy, with hairy legs and eyes on stalks?
Mom: Eat the biscuits and don't worry what's in the tin.

Father: Why did you put a toad in your sister's bed?
Son: I couldn't find a spider.

Witch: I'd like some tiles for my bathroom.
Shopkeeper: But this is a pet shop.
Witch: That's all right – I want reptiles.

Did you hear about the stupid snake?
He lost his skin.

Did you hear about the stupid woodworm?
He was found in a brick.

Did you hear about the glow-worm that didn't know if it was coming or glowing?

Did you hear about the beautiful ancient Greek termite that lunched a thousand ships?

Knock knock.
Who's there?
Thumping.
Thumping who?
Thumping green and slimy is creeping up your leg.

Knock knock.
Who's there?
Maggot.
Maggot who?
Maggot me this new dress today.

Knock knock.
Who's there?
Worm.
Worm who?
Worm in here isn't it?

Knock knock.
Who's there?
Snake.
Snake who?
Snake a move for it!

Knock knock.
Who's there?
Adder.
Adder who?
Adder you get in here?

Knock knock.
Who's there?
Viper.
Viper who?
Viper your nose!

Knock knock.
Who's there?
Python.
Python who?
Python with your pocket money.

Knock knock.
Who's there?
Woodworm.
Woodworm who?
Woodworm cake be enough or
would you like two?

Knock knock.
Who's there?
Crispin.
Crispin who?
Crispin crunchy frog sandwich.

Doctor, doctor, I think I'm turning into a frog.
Oh, you're just playing too much croquet.

Doctor, doctor, I keep thinking I'm a python.
Oh you can't get round me like that, you know.

Doctor, doctor, I keep thinking I'm an adder.
Oh good, could you help me with my tax return?

Doctor, doctor, I keep thinking I'm a toad.
Go on, hop it!

Doctor, doctor, I keep thinking I'm a snail.
Don't worry, we'll soon have you out of your shell.

Doctor, doctor, I feel like an insignificant worm.
Next!

Doctor, doctor, I keep thinking I'm a snake about to shed its skin.
Just slip into something more comfortable.

Waiter, waiter! There's a slug in my salad.
I'm sorry, sir, I didn't know you were a vegetarian.

Waiter, waiter! There's a slug in my dinner.
Don't worry, sir, there's no extra charge.

Waiter, waiter! There's a slug in my lettuce.
Sorry madam, no pets allowed here.

Waiter, waiter! There's a worm in my soup.
That's not a worm, sir, that's your sausage.

Waiter, waiter! There are two worms on my plate.
Those are your sausages, sir.

Waiter, waiter! Do you serve snails?
Sit down, sir, we'll serve anyone.

Waiter, waiter! Have you got frogs' legs?
No, sir, I always walk like this.

Waiter, waiter! Do you have frogs' legs?
Yes sir. Well then hop into the kitchen for my soup.

Waiter, waiter! Are there snails on the menu?
Oh yes, sir, they must have escaped from the kitchen.

243

Waiter, waiter! I can't eat this meat, it's crawling with maggots. Quick, run to the other end of the table, you can catch it as it goes by.

A woman walked into a pet shop and said, "I'd like a frog for my son."
"Sorry madam," said the shopkeeper. "We don't do part exchange."

A blind rabbit and a blind snake ran into each other on the road one day. The snake reached out, touched the rabbit and said, "You're soft and fuzzy and have floppy ears. You must be a rabbit." The rabbit reached out, touched the snake and said, "You're slimy, beady-eyed and low to the ground. You must be a math teacher."

What did the witch say to the ugly
toad?
I'd put a curse on you – but
somebody beat me to it!

What were the only creatures not to
go into the ark in pairs?
Maggots. They went in an apple.

What do you get if you cross a frog with a decathelete?
Someone who pole-vaults without a pole.

1st Witch: I like your toad. He always has such a nice expression on his face.
2nd Witch: It's because he's a hoptimist.

Spook: Should you eat spiders and slugs and zombie slime on an empty stomach?

Witch: No, you should eat them on a plate.

Witch: I'd like a new frog, please.

Pet Shop Assistant: But you bought one only yesterday. What happened?

Witch: It Kermit-ted suicide.